Me and the Weirdos

Me and the Weirdos

JANE SUTTON

Illustrated by Sandy Kossin

Houghton Mifflin Company   Boston   1981

Library of Congress Cataloging in Publication Data

Sutton, Jane.
     Me and the weirdos.

     SUMMARY: Ten-year-old Cindy, constantly embarrassed
by her "weird" parents, finally learns to accept and
appreciate their uniqueness.
     [1. Parent and child — Fiction.   2. Family life —
Fiction.   3. Individuality — Fiction]   I. Title.
PZ7.S96824Me   [Fic]   80-26584
ISBN 0-395-30447-4

To my parents, with love.

Thanks for three decades of hugs, pot roasts and weirdness in moderation.

Contents

Me and the Weirdos

"Mom, Do You Think Our Family is Weird?"

When I was little, I thought everybody's family was like mine.

I didn't notice my family was weird until Roger Snooterman pointed it out to me. Roger is the paper boy in our neighborhood.

One day last spring, Roger came to drop off a bill. He rang our doorbell. It played the first seven notes of "Somewhere Over the Rainbow."

Just as I answered the door, my mother jogged through the front hall with her radio earphones on.

"What in the world is your mother doing, Cindy?" Roger asked.

"She always jogs inside the house," I said. "That's how she gets exercise."

"Your family is really weird," Roger said.

"They are not," I said.

"They are too!" Roger said. "Your mother is the

only grown-up I know who wears red sneakers every day — in summer and winter. Even when it rains, you can see her red sneakers under her see-through galoshes."

"So what?" I said.

"So what?" answered Roger. "You ought to be embarrassed by the things your family does. Your father is the only person in Chesterville who rides a bicycle with an umbrella on it. And his bicycle horn plays the first four notes of 'Frère Jacques.' Tell me that's not weird!"

"The umbrella keeps the rain and sun off his head," I said. "And the horn lets people know he's coming."

"People hear him coming anyway because he's always singing opera," Roger said.

"He likes to sing opera," I said. "Especially on his bicycle."

Roger rolled his eyes. "And let's not forget your sister," he said with a sneer. "Who else rides to school on roller skates and twirls a baton at the same time?"

"I don't know," I said. "I never thought about it before."

"Well, I have," Roger said. "Nobody acts like your family. I know all kinds of families because I deliver papers all over town. And believe me, yours is the weirdest."

With that last "compliment," Roger rode off on his bicycle. "Maybe there will be a weird family contest," he shouted. "Your family might win a free trip or something."

Roger Snooterman thought he was so smart just because he was a couple of years older than I was and just because he was chosen Paper Boy of the Year two years in a row by the *Chesterville News.* But he did know an awful lot of families, and I couldn't help thinking about what he had said.

After he left, I thought about my family. First, I thought about their names. My family's last name *is* pretty weird — it's Krinkle. My father's first name is usually a last name. His first name is Smith.

My mother's name is Squirrel. Before she was married, her first name was Crystal. But she didn't like the way Crystal Krinkle sounded, so she changed her name to Squirrel Krinkle.

I decided to ask Squirrel Krinkle herself about what Roger Snooterman had said. I found my mother polishing the drinking fountain that's in our living room. I took a good look at her. Her frizzy gray hair was sticking straight out, as usual. And of course, she was wearing red sneakers.

"Mom, do you think our family is weird?" I asked her.

"Of course not," she said. "We're a wonderful family!" Then she went on to clean the gumball

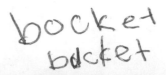

machine next to the drinking fountain. I wondered what Roger Snooterman would say about the way our living room is furnished.

I decided to talk to my father too. I found him working in the backyard.

I had to admit that my father didn't look like your everyday person. The top of his head is completely bald, but he has long black hair that starts about an inch above his ears and hangs down in a scraggly mess almost to his shoulders.

He was planting dandelion seeds.

My father has a collection of all kinds of weeds growing in our backyard. Our yard also has about 50 million birdfeeders that he made out of coconuts and old beer cans. And he trimmed the hedges in the front yard in the shape of two penguins and three rocket ships.

While my father planted dandelion seeds, I said to him, "My friend Patti's father kills the dandelions in *his* yard with chemicals. Don't you think it's kind of weird to grow dandelions on purpose?"

"Not at all," he said. "Dandelions are very pretty. Especially compared to dull, ordinary grass. Grass is always the same old green, except when it turns brown, and no one likes brown grass."

I looked around the yard and I thought that my father's weeds were kind of pretty. A lot of them had colorful flowers. But I figured that Roger Snooterman would say it was weird to go out of your way to grow plants that most people try to kill.

I decided to ask my sister, Sarah, what she thought about our family.

Sarah collects things. Some big sisters collect stamps or coins or autographs. My friend Patti's big sister used to collect posters of famous singers. But *my* big sister collects can labels. She especially likes labels from cans of mixed vegetables and cans of creamed corn.

My mother hardly ever serves canned food, so Sarah has to go around asking people for empty cans to get the labels. Then she papers her room with them.

I knocked on the door of Sarah's room.

"Who desires entrance and what is your purpose?" Sarah shouted — her usual greeting.

"It's me," I said. "I want to ask you something. Do you think our family is weird?"

There was no answer.

"Sarah!" I shouted. "Did you hear me?"

"Don't bother me," she answered. "I'm counting my baked bean labels."

What a family! I thought. My mother was polishing the gumball machine in our living room, my father was planting weeds, and my sister was counting baked bean labels.

I decided that Roger Snooterman was right. My family was weird.

The more I thought about it, the more I agreed with Roger. My father, for example, picks you up and twirls you around in a circle when he's glad to see you. Not everyone likes it.

My mother gargles with orange juice three times a day. She says it makes her feel refreshed. My sister has bright red curly hair that looks like a red bird's nest. She's only thirteen and she's almost as tall as my father.

Our family even has a weird pet. We don't have a cat or a dog or a parakeet. We have a sea urchin. His name is Gomer. He's a little gray, round thing with spines all over him, and his mouth is in the middle of his bottom.

Sarah found Gomer at the beach on a school field trip last year. She made a big deal about how we should have a pet. She promised to change his water and add salt to it and feed him seaweed and hamburgers, and she does.

Gomer usually sits around in a bowl all day. If you take him out of his bowl to play with him, you have to be very careful because his spines are sharp. Sea urchins usually don't have much personality, and Gomer is no exception.

I wondered if I was as weird as the rest of my family. But, even though I went along with some of the things my family did, I decided that I was not weird. I'm a normal ten-year-old girl. I work hard at school. I like to draw pictures and play the piano. I dress neatly, and I have long brown hair that I usually wear with two barrettes. I have brown eyes and some freckles on my nose. You could never guess from looking at me that I live with a bunch of weirdos.

I wondered how many people besides Roger Snooterman knew I had a weird family. I wondered if I would lose all my friends if they found out.

I decided I had better do something fast. Trying to talk to my family hadn't helped. So I decided to try not talking to them.

My plan was to start not talking the next day. I figured that after a while, someone would ask me why I was so quiet. I would say, "Because you're all so weird. And if you don't quit being weird, I'll *never* talk to you again."

For breakfast the next day, my mother made pancakes. She makes delicious pancakes. And they're in different shapes because she pours the batter into cookie cutters on the hot frying pan. We usually eat them topped with fresh fruit, except for Sarah, who tops them with tomato sauce.

Anyway, the idea of those fabulous pancakes just *got* to me, I guess. When my mother asked me if I wanted fresh strawberries with them, I said, "I'd love some," before I remembered I was supposed to be silent.

The duck-shaped pancakes with butter and fresh strawberries made having a weird family a little easier to swallow.

There must be another way to get them to change, I thought as I reached for a second helping.

The Impossible Homework Assignment

The next few days I was very busy in school. So I didn't think much about how to stop my family from being weird.

One day, my teacher, Mrs. Reed, gave us a difficult homework assignment. The assignment wasn't so hard for the rest of the class. But it was just about impossible for me.

We were supposed to watch a TV program that night and write a review of it in class the next day. Mrs. Reed told us to take notes while we watched. She told us to write down the names of the actors and actresses and the roles they played, and the names of the director and the producer. She told us to jot down what happened on the show and what the scenery was like.

When we wrote the review, we were supposed to use our notes to write about the show, and then tell if we liked it and why or why not.

Everybody in my class was excited about the assignment.

"I'm gonna watch 'Journey to the Planet Zetto,'" my friend Grant said.

"I think I'll watch 'The Bob and Bobby Show,'" a girl in my class named Brenda said.

It seemed that everybody was looking forward to writing about their favorite shows. Except for me. The whole thing was impossible for me because my family doesn't have a TV set! Some kids in my class have three TVs. My friend Patti's family has two color sets and a black-and-white. We don't even have one crummy black-and-white set.

My parents say it's bad for you to sit and stare at TV. They say it's better to be doing things yourself than to watch people on TV doing things. I never made a big deal about not having a TV. It had never seemed important before. We do have a record player and a radio. And I can watch two TVs when I go to Patti's.

I go to Patti's house lots of days after school. She and I do just about everything together, except she belongs to the Young Raccoons and I belong to the Young Blue Jays. You might say that Patti is my best friend.

Patti has short blonde hair with bangs. *She*'s kind of short too. She's cute. Patti is really nice and funny and she is smart in school. Her family is nice and normal. But for some reason, she likes to hang around with my family.

After we got the TV review assignment, I went straight home. My mother was giving fencing lessons in our basement so I had to wait for her students to leave before I could tell her about it. She teaches fencing three days a week.

"What an interesting assignment," she said.

"But I can't do it," I said.

"Why not?" she asked.

"Because we don't have a TV," I said.

"We don't?" she asked. "Oh, I guess you're right."

My mother doesn't have such a great memory. She says that she's too busy doing things in the present to think about the past. But I reminded her that it was right now, in the present, that we didn't have a TV.

"Why don't you watch TV at a friend's house tonight?" she asked.

"Because Mrs. Reed wants us to watch by ourselves," I explained. "That way, we'll all watch different shows. And we won't have a chance to tell each other what we think of the shows before we write our reviews."

"That makes sense," my mother said. She poured a glass of orange juice and started gargling. She threw back her head and made noises like a chicken with a bad headache.

"What am I going to do about watching TV?" I asked when she finished gargling.

"TV?" she said. "Oh, well, since it's for a school assignment, we'll just have to rent one."

She called Rent-a-Thing and arranged to rent a color TV set. My father picked it up on his way home from work. He rode home with the TV strapped to his bicycle.

My father rides his bike to work every day, even when it snows. He works at the airport, which is about ten miles from our house. His job is to clean airplanes between flights. He likes his job because he works alone, and no one is there to complain about his off-key opera singing.

My father brings home those air-sickness bags they give you on airplanes, for me and Sarah to carry our lunches in. Sarah actually takes her lunch to school in those bags. I don't.

I decided to watch a TV special called "Comedy Corner." When it was time for the show, I got a notebook and pencil to take notes. I turned on the TV and sat down on a mattress. Our living room has mattresses all over the floor instead of sofas and chairs. I waited for the TV to come on, but nothing happened.

"Daddy!" I called. "Nothing's happening."

"I think you have to let TVs warm up," he said. He was in the dining room, singing opera and watering pots of crabgrass he had just transplanted from the yard.

I waited a while longer. Then I said, "Dad! It's still not on. I'm going to miss the beginning of the show."

He came into the living room and turned the On/Off button off and then on again. Nothing happened. He turned the channel selector to every channel, from 1 to 13. But nothing happened. He adjusted the antenna. But still nothing happened.

"I'm going to miss the show, and I won't be able to do the assignment," I said. I almost started to cry. My father went to get his safari hat. He has one of those tan hats that explorers wear in the jungle. He claims that it helps him think better because it keeps thoughts from flying away. He looks good in the hat because it hides the top of his bald head. When you just see his long black hair, it makes you think he has hair on the top of his head too.

My mother and Sarah came into the living room and sat down on mattresses. When I told them the TV wouldn't go on, my mother went to call Rent-a-Thing for advice. My father paced around the living room with his safari hat on, looking at the TV every once in a while.

Just as my mother came back, my father threw

his hat up in the air and said, "I've got it!" He ran over to the TV and plugged it in. It went on right away. We all shouted, "Yay!"

"What did Rent-a-Thing say?" Sarah asked my mother.

"The manager asked me if we had the TV plugged in," said my mother. "I told him, 'Of course we do.'"

We all laughed. I felt better now that I could watch most of the ninety-minute special.

"I'm going to call Rent-a-Thing back," my mother said.

"Why?" Sarah asked her.

"Ssh," I said. "I'm trying to listen to the show."

"I want to tell the manager the TV wasn't plugged in after all," my mother said. My mother is very honest. She doesn't believe in any kind of lying. She wanted to tell Rent-a-Thing the TV wasn't plugged in, even though she really thought it was plugged in when she said so.

There was a skit on the TV special about a doughnut shop that only served doughnut holes. Customers were ordering strawberry jelly holes and sugar holes and plain holes. It was cute. I wrote down some of the jokes in my notebook, and I wrote down which characters I thought were the funniest.

My father said, "You know, a shop that serves doughnut holes is a good idea."

"It's supposed to be funny, Dad," I said.

"How come you're talking?" Sarah asked me. "I thought you have to listen to the show."

I didn't bother to answer her.

My mother came back in and said, "Some people! I called Rent-a-Thing and told the manager that the TV hadn't been plugged in after all. He said, 'Who cares?' Some people just don't appreciate honesty."

I wished everyone would be quiet so I could watch the show. When a commercial came on, my father turned the volume down so low that you couldn't hear it. He said he didn't want Sarah and me to listen to commercials. He said that commercials make you think you need things you'd be better off not having — like cereal made with a lot of sugar and poorly made toys that break the first time you play with them. He said commercials can talk you into anything.

"I know a stewardess who watched a cat food commercial," he said. "The commercial had a singing cat. She liked it so much, she ran out and bought a whole case of cat food. She doesn't even have a cat."

There was a commercial on the TV about a hamburger restaurant. It looked really funny without any sound. You could see people singing away and no sound was coming out of their mouths. Sarah started making up a jingle — "Our hamburgers are so delicious . . . and so nutritious . . . we make them quick . . . but you'll get sick!"

There was another commercial about an allergy medicine. A man was holding a bottle of the pills and talking. My father started talking as the man's lips moved. "This allergy medicine is great," he said. "It really . . . achoo . . . makes me . . . achoo . . . feel much . . . achoo . . . better."

When the show came back on, I started to turn up the volume. But Sarah said, "Let's leave the sound off. I want to make up my own words some more."

"I have to listen to the show for homework," I said.

"Just one skit," Sarah said. "It's so much fun!"

"O.K.," I said. "Just one."

There was a skit on about people camping in the wilderness. Sarah and my parents acted it out. My mother made noises like a wolf. Sarah talked along with the little girl in the skit. My father made up the words for one of the frightened campers. He really looked like a camper with his safari hat.

When the next skit came on, I tried to turn up the volume again. "Oh, don't be a drag," Sarah said.

"I let you act out one skit," I said. "Now turn the sound back on . . ."

"No!" Sarah said. She stood in front of the TV.

"Yes!" I said. I tried to reach around her, but she pushed me away.

"Girls, girls, a little less violence," my father said.

I tried to push Sarah out of the way to get to the volume button. She wouldn't let me near it. We pushed each other a couple more times and somehow the TV got knocked over. It fell on the floor. Crash! We could hear something fall apart on the inside.

My father lifted the TV off the floor. The picture was still on. He turned the volume button, but nothing happened. He turned the button all the way, but still nothing happened. The sound was broken!

"Now look what you did," I said to Sarah.

"What *I* did!" shouted Sarah. "You're the one . . ."

"Stop fighting, girls," my mother said. "Now you see what violence and TV lead to."

"Ha ha," Sarah said. "We'll *have* to act out skits without the sound now. We *can't* turn the sound on."

"Sarah's right," my father said. "We may as well have fun acting out skits."

"Can't you fix the sound?" I asked him.

"If I start taking the TV apart to fix the volume, you'll miss the rest of the show," he said. "I'll have to fix it later. You can still watch the show even though you can't listen."

While my weirdo parents and sister started acting out skits, I took notes about the scenery and costumes.

"Why don't you join in too, Cindy?" my mother asked.

"It's not every day that we have a TV," my father said. "Why don't you act along with us in between taking notes?"

"I don't feel like it," I said. I sat on a mattress and scowled. I worried about how I could write my review without having heard the show. If Roger Snooterman were there, he would have said, "I told you so."

The next skit was about a hospital.

"I'm afraid we'll have to operate on your zookalooloo bone," Sarah said when the nurse was on the screen.

"Oh no!" said my father when there was a close-up of the patient.

"Not the zookalooloo bone!" said my mother, the patient's wife.

My family acted out three more skits and five more commercials. They kept asking me to join in too, but I wouldn't.

The last skit was about astronauts going to the moon. Sarah and my mother were the astronauts.

My father was in the control station. "Ten, nine, eight, seven, six . . ." he said.

"What can I bring you from the moon?" my mother asked my father before she blasted off.

"Some green cheese," my father said. "Five, four, three, two, one, zero, Blastoff!"

"Oh no, I forgot my label collection," Sarah the astronaut said as the rocket ship blasted off on TV.

When the show was over, I copied down the names of the cast that flashed on the screen. I couldn't get them all written down because they went by too fast.

My mother and father and Sarah went down to the basement because it was nine o'clock. Every night, from nine to nine-fifteen, they scream together. They think it's a good way to get rid of any bad feelings left over from the day. I used to do it too. But after I found out they were weird, I started playing the piano from nine to nine-fifteen to drown out the screams. We have a grand piano in our kitchen.

I felt like screaming too when I thought about my homework assignment. But I didn't. I just sat on one of the living room mattresses and worried.

The next day in school, I told Patti what had happened. I knew I could trust her not to tell anyone about the things my family did.

"It's too bad you and Sarah had a fight," Patti said.

"But acting out the skits sounds like fun. *My* parents just sat there and watched the show with me. It was dull city." (*City* is one of Patti's favorite words. She says things are dull city, super city, bad city, and lots of other cities. Patti is pretty great city, in my opinion.)

I said to her, "Things would be a lot easier if my family were dull city. How can I write my review when I didn't hear the show?"

"Write what you *did* hear," Patti said. "I bet what your family said was better than the show anyway."

"Mrs. Reed won't think so," I said. "She told us to listen to the show and take notes."

"You tried to listen," Patti said. "Wait . . . I have an idea. You could write a review about what it's like to watch TV without the sound."

"Mrs. Reed will send me to the school psychologist if she reads that," I said. But I did take Patti's advice because she's pretty smart in school and because I couldn't think of any other way out.

I wrote what I saw on TV and what I heard from my family. I wrote about the scenery and the costumes and I wrote what my family said. I didn't mention the fight. At the end of the review, I really got carried away. I wrote that watching TV without the sound is a new form of family entertainment. "It helps develop your imagination," I wrote.

Before I handed in my review, I scribbled down the title: "A TV Show Plus More." I hoped for the best.

Mrs. Reed read our reviews while we were in gym. She handed them back at the end of the day. Mine said: "Excellent! Good details and funny. I'd love to meet your family, Cindy."

She won't meet my family if I can help it, I thought. I liked Mrs. Reed and I didn't want her to see all the other crazy things my family does. Besides, I figured that she didn't mean what she wrote anyway. She probably wrote those nice things just because she felt sorry for someone in such a weird family.

3

How to Unweird a Family

I decided that having a weird family was causing me much too much trouble. Roger Snooterman was right. They were just plain embarrassing.

I made up my mind to think of a plan to get them to stop being weird. Talking to them hadn't worked. And my silence plan hadn't lasted through one pancakes-with-strawberries breakfast.

I decided to try something new. I thought that if my family tried acting normal, they might like it and decide to make it a habit.

The next Saturday, my father was busy planting dandelions and crabgrass in the front yard. My mother was trimming the rocket ship and penguin hedges. Sarah was twirling her baton while she roller-skated in the driveway. It was an unusually warm day for May.

I sat on the front steps trying to think of a normal activity for my family to do. I figured that being with other people might help. Maybe they stayed weird because they hung around together too much without seeing normal people.

I saw a family go by in a station wagon. The kids in the back had pails, shovels, rubber rafts, and flippers.

The beach! I thought. I couldn't remember ever going to the beach with my family. I went to Patti's parents' swimming pool club lots of times. Everybody acted normal there . . .

I figured that the beach would be a perfect place to unweird my family — they would be surrounded by normal people. They couldn't help learning to act normal!

I ran into the front yard. "Let's go to the beach," I said.

My father got into one of his big-word moods: "You, Cindy, are a true inspiration," he said. "There is nothing quite so lovely as the beach — the magic place where land meets water. And incidentally, my increasing perspiration as I labor with these plants makes the idea additionally appealing."

"I haven't been to the beach in years," said my mother. She threw down her pruning shears. "Let's go," she said.

My mother told Sarah that we were going to the

beach. We all changed into our beach clothes. Then we piled into our van, which has a big painting of a rainbow on the outside.

We were about to leave when my mother said, "Wait a minute!" She jumped out of the van and ran around it three times. While she ran, she flapped her elbows like a bird and made crowing noises. Luckily, we were in our own driveway. I don't think anyone saw her.

When she got back in the van, she said, "Now we should have good weather at the beach. That was a sun dance one of my fencing students taught me."

On the way to the beach, we saw a teenage girl hitchhiking.

My father pulled over to pick her up. She climbed into the van, saying, "Thanks a lot!" Then she looked around and got very quiet. She looked kind of scared.

I didn't blame her for being scared. I saw her look at my father. He had his safari hat on to keep the sun off the bald top of his head. His arms were covered with tattoos he had painted with watercolors. The tattoos on his left arm were pictures of animals. Along his right arm, he had painted, "Have you hugged an airplane cleaner today?"

I saw the hitchhiker look at my mother. My mother doesn't have a bathing suit. So she was wearing a pink ballerina tutu and, of course, her red sneakers. Her gray frizzy hair was sticking out more than ever.

The hitchhiker took a quick glance behind her at Sarah. She was wearing a straw hat over her bright red hair and a white karate suit to keep the sun off her fair skin.

I had a normal bathing suit on. But I guess one normal person can't cancel out three weirdos. The hitchhiker stared straight ahead, out the windshield. Her lips were moving a little. Maybe she was praying.

My father gave the hitchhiker a lecture. He told her she shouldn't hitchhike. "You never know what kind of strange people will pick you up," he said.

"I know what you mean," said the hitchhiker.

When we got to the beach, the hitchhiker started to rush out of the van. "Wait just a minute," my father said.

The hitchhiker kept her hand on the door handle and listened.

"I don't want you hitchhiking anymore," said my father.

"Oh, I won't," the hitchhiker said. "I promise."

"Here's money to rent a bicycle to ride home," my father said. "There's a bike rental shop near the snack bar."

The hitchhiker stared at him. Then she stuffed the money into her pocket and said, "Thanks." She got out of the van and ran toward the beach.

My family just may have cured her of hitchhiking.

"Rats!" said my father. "I should have told her to look for a bicycle with an umbrella on it."

We got a good spot on the beach, right near the water. I was hoping my family would look around and get an idea of what you're supposed to do at the beach. People were wading, sunbathing, listening to radios, playing cards, throwing Frisbees . . .

"Who wants to play catch?" I asked my family. "I brought along a beach ball. We can throw it around and maybe some other people will play with us."

"Maybe later," said my father. "I want to fly my kite now."

He started flying this weird kite he had made. It looks like a hamburger. In fact, he calls it The Flying Hamburger.

My mother didn't want to play catch either. She was busy practicing cartwheels in the sand.

Sarah just wanted to read the dictionary she had brought. She sat in the sun with her karate suit on. I know she has to protect her skin from the sun, but did she have to wear mittens and take them off each time she turned the page?

I could feel people on the beach staring at us. I would have liked to bury my head in the sand. But I lay on the beach blanket and pretended to be enjoying the sun.

After a while, I heard a commotion. I looked up and saw my father struggling with The Flying Hamburger. It had fallen on a Frisbee player and the Frisbee player was tangled up in the string. When the Frisbee player got untangled, he and the three other players moved to another part of the beach.

My father put away The Flying Hamburger.

"How about going wading?" I suggested. The water was too cold for swimming.

"Yes, let's try out the Queen Miranda," said my mother.

My father said, "Aye aye, Captain."

I hadn't realized that my mother had brought along her toy boat. It was bad enough that she played with the Queen Miranda at home in the bathtub. But now she was going to play with it on a public beach where everyone could see her! I decided I didn't want to go in the water with my parents after all.

My mother and father put the boat in the water. They giggled as it got tossed around in the waves.

They made lots of noise being enthusiastic. "There it goes!" they shouted. "Oops, it almost sank! Whee!"

I tried to read a book. But I couldn't concentrate on it. I kept reading the same paragraph.

After a while, I gave up reading and looked around. I counted fourteen people sitting near us. Fourteen, plus four Frisbee players, plus one hitchhiker — that made nineteen more people who now knew that my family was weird. This beach outing was not working out as I had wanted it to.

I looked at the family next to us. There was a grandmother playing with a baby. The mother and father were sitting in beach chairs and reading newspapers. They all wore normal bathing suits. Why couldn't my family be normal, like them?

The people on the other side of us were cooking hot dogs and hamburgers. They had the right idea — they were going to eat hamburgers, not fly one! There was a mother and a father and a boy and a girl. I wished my family were as normal as that family. They even had a normal-looking dog. They probably didn't have any dumb sea urchin at home.

I asked Sarah if she wanted to help me dig a big hole and bury each other in it. It seemed like a pretty normal thing to do at the beach.

She wouldn't even look up from her dictionary.

"Don't bother me," she said. "I want to finish the B's today."

My parents were still playing with the Queen Miranda. At least my father's watercolor tattoos had washed off in the water. But he still had that safari hat on with his long, scraggly hair hanging down from it. And my mother had that ballerina outfit.

"Hey, Cindy, come play with the boat!" my mother, the beach ballerina, shouted.

Quickly, I lay down and pretended to be asleep. No one could tell she was talking to me if I didn't answer.

I guess my parents got tired of the boat after a while. I heard my father say, "I think I will embark on a walk. A walk on the beach is enormously exhilarating."

My mother lay down on the beach blanket next to me. "My sun dance must have worked," she said. "The weather is beautiful — you already have some new freckles on your nose, Cindy."

I didn't say anything. She seemed to fall asleep and I fell asleep too. I had a dream that Roger Snooterman was on the beach laughing and pointing at me.

When I woke up, my mother was packing up the Queen Miranda and The Flying Hamburger. "It must be getting late," she said. "I'm starved." My mother never wears a watch. She goes on stomach time.

"Where's Daddy?" I asked.

"He hasn't gotten back from his walk yet," my mother said.

Sarah started calling, "Daddy-O! Daddy-cakes!"

"Can't you just call him Daddy?" I asked. My face felt red. And it wasn't just from sunburn.

"Don't be silly," Sarah said. "If I yelled 'Daddy,' every father on the beach would turn around."

As far as I could tell, every father on the beach *was* turning to look at her. And so was every mother, sister, brother, aunt, and uncle.

Then we heard a loud voice. It was the lifeguard talking over his bullhorn. "Attention, please!" he said. "I have a lost man here. He's about forty-five years old . . ."

We looked at the lifeguard, and there was my father standing on the big chair behind him.

"He's wearing a safari hat . . ." the lifeguard said.

"Smith!" my mother shouted.

"And he answers to the name of Smith Krinkle," the lifeguard said.

My mother ran toward the lifeguard chair. When my father saw her, he waved and climbed down. He and my mother hugged. He picked her up and whirled her around because he was glad to see her.

Everybody on the beach laughed and cheered.

"I couldn't remember where our blanket was," my father explained.

I thought, *I am mortified.* I wasn't sure if *mortified* was the right word for the way I felt. While Sarah jumped up and down and cheered, I looked it up in her dictionary. It said: "*Mortify* — To hurt someone's pride or self-respect." I was mortified all right.

We got ready to leave. I was grateful for one thing — we hadn't run into anyone we knew.

4

Foreign Behavior

You would think that a day on the beach with my family would be enough mortification for me. But sometimes when I get an idea in my head, I can't let go of it. So I didn't give up my unweirding plan. I still hoped that my family might give up their weird ways if they gave being normal a fair chance.

I stayed on the lookout for unweirding activities. Pretty soon, a perfect opportunity came up. At school, Mrs. Reed handed out a notice asking families to volunteer to have a foreign student stay with them. Chesterville had a chance to have a student from France for two weeks in June if a host family could be found.

I wanted my family to volunteer. I figured that hosting a foreign student would be a nice, normal thing for them to do. Even *they* would know to be on their best behavior in front of a foreign visitor, I figured.

For the plan to work, they would only have to be unweird for two weeks at first. If things worked out, it might just put them on the road to being normal. The next time, they could try being normal for three weeks, and then maybe forever.

When I brought home the notice, my father was very enthusiastic. He got into a big-word mood. "Excellent! Excellent!" he said. "The interweaving of international culture is a wonderful concept to explore."

My mother thought it would be nice to meet someone from another country.

Sarah asked with a sneer, "Where is this French student going to sleep?"

"In your room," said my mother. "Your room is bigger than Cindy's."

"I don't like people near my can labels," Sarah said. "I won't be able to watch this stranger every minute. The last time someone was in my room without me, there were six creamed corn labels missing afterwards."

"Sarah, my dear," my father said. "I think it's wonderful that you have developed your own original hobby. And I think it's excellent that you train your eyes to notice the barely noticeable differences among can labels. But I think you exaggerate the interest that other people have in your collection."

"In other words," I said, "no one is going to steal your labels because no one cares about your dumb collection."

"Well, I'm totally against our hosting a student," Sarah said.

That's how I knew I was totally for it. Sarah and I disagree about almost everything. So if she was against it, I knew it must be O.K.

The French student who was coming to our house was named Marguerite. We all went to the airport in the rainbow van to pick her up. On the way, I asked my family, "You'll all be on your best behavior, right?"

"We'll show Marguerite a wonderful time," my mother said. "Because we're a wonderful family."

The first thing my father did when we got to the airport was put on his French beret. It pressed his hair down, so his black, stringy hair looked even longer than usual.

"What are you doing?" I asked him.

"I want to make Marguerite feel at home," he said.

Marguerite's flight was right on time. She found us at the information booth, where we had arranged to meet her. She looked very nice but shy. "Allo," she said. She had a French accent.

I shook her hand and said hello.

My mother gave her a bear hug that could knock you out for a month. My father picked her up and twirled her around in a circle.

I thought Marguerite would want to get right back on the plane. But she acted as if everything was O.K. She even smiled a little.

Sarah asked her, "How come they call french fries 'french fries'?"

"Excuse me," Marguerite said. "I don't understand what you mean."

"I think french fries is an American name," my mother said. "I also think we should go home now. Marguerite must be very tired and hungry."

I was glad my mother was acting so sensibly. I gave Sarah a dirty look. But it was lost on her. She was busy bothering my father about why they never put french fries in cans.

Back at the house, we ate dinner. My mother had cooked a vegetable stew. As usual, we all ate out of one pot. The pot sits in the middle of the table and we eat from it with wooden spoons that have extra-long handles. My parents think it makes us a close family to eat dinner out of one pot.

Marguerite didn't say anything about our weird eating arrangement. "Thees stew is very much de-

leecious," she said. "What are some of the things
that are in it?"

"I don't remember," my mother said. "Let me
look . . . I see potatoes . . . onions . . . peppers,
tomatoes, turnips, celery, parsley . . . There seems
to be just about every vegetable you could think of
in there, except broccoli."

"You don't eat broccoli in thees countree?" Marguerite asked.

"Broccoli has so much personality that it seems
mean to eat it," my mother said.

After dinner, my parents suggested one of their
favorite activities — painting pictures on the living

room wall. Most parents hang paintings in frames on their walls. Or they might have a sculpture or a weaving. But *my* family paints right on the wall.

We used to have a painting of a jungle with lots of animals and crazy-looking trees. Then we had a city painting with skyscrapers and buses and bridges. We change the painting about three times a year. We just paint over it with white paint and start a new one.

I used to enjoy painting on the wall before I found out my family was weird. But now I didn't want any part of it.

My father put plastic sheets on everything in the living room — the mattresses, the water fountain, and the gumball machine. He had painted the wall white to get ready for Marguerite's visit.

"You are going to paint on the wall?" Marguerite asked.

"Mais oui!" said my father. That means "But yes!" in French. "What would you like to paint?" he asked her.

"Maybe she doesn't feel like painting on the wall," I said. "Why don't we go to the movies? There's a nice family movie playing at the Chester-ville Cinema. It's rated PG."

"I would love to paint," Marguerite said. "I just don't know *what* to paint."

My father knew what *he* wanted to paint. We all

watched while he started painting something very tall. It was skinny on the top and fatter on the bottom. He used black paint.

"The Eiffel Tower!" Marguerite said.

"Mais oui!" said my father. "Let's all paint some scenes of France."

My mother painted a French bakery with lots of French breads. Sarah painted a grocery store with cans in the window that said "French onion soup" and "French style green beans." Marguerite painted her house back home.

Since everybody was acting weird anyway, I decided to paint on the wall too. I painted a sign that said "Welcome Marguerite" along the top of the wall.

"Oh, thank you, Cindee," Marguerite said when she saw it.

I kept thinking how odd she must have thought my family was. She was very polite though. She acted as if she enjoyed the painting.

At nine o'clock, it was time for the nightly screaming session. By then, I figured Marguerite must have thought my family was really nuts. But she seemed to think screaming was a good idea. She even joined in.

Then she took a shower in our outdoor shower. The shower is in our backyard. Its sides are made out of an old milk truck.

After her shower, Marguerite settled into the extra bed in Sarah's room. Sarah made her promise not to touch any of her can labels.

I wondered if you could get fired from being a host family.

The rest of Marguerite's stay went by really fast. Every day after school, we took her sightseeing. We went to parks and museums. At night, we went to the movies and to the best restaurants in Chesterville.

My family didn't act weird too often. And when they did, Marguerite would say, "How interesting!"

Sometimes we listened to records and pretended we were playing different instruments in the orchestra. That's one of my family's favorite things to do. Marguerite seemed to like it too.

She also came with me to one of my Young Blue Jay meetings. My Young Blue Jay group meets once a week. We do all kinds of normal things. We sew, we put on plays, we go on hikes, and do lots of other stuff. Marguerite talked to the Young Blue Jays about life in France. She liked them and they liked her.

School was lots of fun while Marguerite stayed with us. Everybody wanted to know what it was like to host a foreign student. Mrs. Reed made a big deal about how nice my family was to volunteer for the program.

We had lots of visitors at our house while Marguerite was around. My friend Grant came over twice after school. Patti came out to a restaurant with us one night. Another night, her parents came over to show us their slides of France.

Even Roger Snooterman stopped in to chat when he delivered the paper. Luckily, my parents were reading in the living room (almost like normal parents, except that they were sitting on mattresses) when he came.

Roger couldn't leave without reminding me what he thought of my family. "I wonder how they let *your* family host a foreign student," he said.

I didn't answer him. It was a good question. But Roger didn't realize that the Krinkles were on the road to being normal.

By the time Marguerite went home, I actually felt my family had done a good job being hosts. Marguerite had had a great time with us. She even cried when she left.

A couple of weeks later, it was my turn to cry. It was summer vacation and I had spent the day at Patti's parents' swimming club. When I got home, Sarah was all excited. She was twirling her baton at about a hundred miles an hour. "We're in the paper," she said.

She turned to page three of the *Chesterville News* and showed me this:

FRENCH STUDENT WRITES ABOUT CHESTERVILLE TRIP

Our French visitor, Marguerite Lyonnet, has sent us an article she wrote for her hometown paper in France. Marguerite was a guest of Mr. and Mrs. Smith Krinkle and family for two weeks last month. Here is the article, translated by Miss Alberta Possum of the Chesterville High School French Department:

"I had a wonderful time in the United States. My host family was so sweet to me!

"I learned many interesting things about Americans. Did you know that they all eat from one pot at dinner? Also, they don't eat broccoli because it seems like a human. When Americans make a peanut-butter sandwich, they put the peanut butter on the outside and the bread on the inside, so you can taste the peanut butter more.

"Every night, the American family gets together and screams. It makes you feel better — I tried it too.

"The American women are very strong. They hug you hard. For exercise, they jog around the house while wearing earphones. To be healthy, they gargle with orange juice.

"The men ride to work on bikes with special umbrellas on them. In the winter, it's too cold to ride bikes, so they ride on exercise bikes indoors while they look at slides of outdoor scenes. Also, the men wear berets, just like in France.

"Americans have showers outside. The children collect can labels. They keep sea urchins for pets.

"Sadly, I didn't have a chance to spend much time with any other American families besides my hosts. But if other Americans are like Smith, Squirrel, Sarah, and Cindy Krinkle in Chesterville, the United States is a very nice and a very different country.

"P.S. To wake them up in the morning, Americans have alarm clocks with a tape recording that says cock-a-doodle-doo."

"Isn't that a neat article?" Sarah asked. "She remembers everything about us."

I didn't answer. I burst into tears.

"Just because she talked about my can label collection and she hardly wrote a word about you is no reason to cry," said Sarah. "You could start an unusual collection too. Why don't you start collecting different color shoelaces?"

I thought, *I'll never get my family to be normal.*

It was bad enough when they acted weird on the beach in front of strangers. But now the whole world (including people I knew) would read how weird they were — at least everybody in Chesterville and everybody in France.

5

One Weirdo at a Time

I felt really terrible about Marguerite's article in the *Chesterville News.* Luckily, the article came out during summer vacation and I didn't have to face anyone at school. I hung around the house so I wouldn't run into anybody.

When Roger Snooterman delivered the paper, I hid in the closet. I knew that if he saw me, he would say that my family had given the French a bad impression of the United States. He would probably say that Chesterville wouldn't be allowed to have any more foreign exchange students and it was all my family's fault.

I didn't even feel like calling Patti. I didn't even go to my next Young Blue Jay meeting. I was afraid one of the Young Blue Jays would laugh at me and say, "I hear you have an alarm clock that says cock-a-doodle-doo."

I knew I couldn't avoid people for the rest of my life. I tried to think of new and improved unweirding plans so I wouldn't have to be embarrassed by my family forever.

A few days after the article appeared, I was out in the backyard throwing a tennis ball against the outdoor shower. It felt good to throw hard, and those metal milk truck walls made a nice, loud noise.

I saw my mother's frizzy gray head pop out the window: "Cindy, you have a visitor," she said.

It was Patti. I noticed she had gotten her bangs cut.

"Oh hi, Patti," I said. I kept throwing the ball against the shower.

"What's wrong?" Patti asked. "You look like sad city."

I looked around to make sure no one else was listening. Then I asked, "Did you see the article in the *Chesterville News?*"

"Yeah," Patti said, and she started to laugh.

"Well that's what's wrong," I said. "My family is so weird!"

"Your family is great!" Patti said. "They're imaginative, they're interesting . . ."

"You don't have to live with them," I said.

"They're the happiest people I ever met," said Patti.

"That's because they're too weird even to know they're weird," I answered.

"Tell the truth," Patti said, "don't you have fun with your family — just a little?"

"No," I said. "Well, not anymore anyway. Not since I found out they're weird. I keep worrying about what other people think of them."

"Well, I may be short, but I *am* another person," said Patti. "And I'm crazy about your family. Other people like them too, even if they are . . . well . . . different."

"How could anyone like people who make peanut-butter sandwiches with the peanut butter on the outside?" I asked.

"How could you not like them?" Patti answered.

We both laughed. I felt a little better, knowing that my best friend still wanted to hang around with me. But I was sure she was the only one who really liked my family.

Then Patti came up with an idea. "If you really get sick of your family," she said, "you can come live with *my* family. We have an extra bedroom now that my sister is married."

"How do you know your parents would want me?" I asked.

"I just know they would," Patti said. "They think you're a real nice kid and they think you have a great sense of humor."

"Well, I don't know if I want to give up on my family yet," I said. "I'm working on a new and improved unweirding plan."

My new idea was to work on my family one weirdo at a time. I decided that it had been a mistake to take on the whole family at once. No wonder going to the beach and hosting a foreign student hadn't worked! You just can't unweird three weirdos together. In my new plan, I would give each person in my family all my attention and unweird them one by one.

I decided to start with my mother. I figured that once she was normal, she could help me unweird my father. And when he was normal too, both of them could help me work on Sarah . . .

A few days later, my mother came down with a cold. If you think my mother is strange when she's well, you should see her when she's sick.

The morning she got sick, she and I were alone in the house. My father was at work and Sarah was at a baton-twirling clinic at the junior high.

I decided I would teach my mother to be sick like everybody else.

"You need plenty of rest," I told her.

Her nose was stuffed up, so her answer sounded like this: "I doe it, Ciddy. You're right."

She got into bed and said she would stay there until she was better. She promised me that she wouldn't jog around the house, and she canceled all her fencing classes for the rest of the day.

I thought I was making progress.

"When you have a cold, you should drink a lot," I told her.

"Yes, you're right," she said. She promised to gargle with orange juice every fifteen minutes. I figured gargling was almost the same as drinking.

"How about taking a cold pill?" I suggested. "The last time I was at Patti's, I saw this TV commercial for Cold-Away Pills. They soothe colds in six different ways."

"Oh, I have better rebedies thad pills," she said.

I left her alone to rest. I went into my room and wrote a letter to Grant, who was away at summer camp.

After a while, I went in to check on my patient. I hadn't been gone long at all, but she was already back to her weird ways. She was lying in bed wearing her special "sick hat" — it's made out of wads of cotton. She claims it helps headaches. She was looking at restful pictures — of cows and cats lying down — to make herself feel peaceful.

She had moved the weed plants from the dining room around her bed. She thinks they help her breathe better. And she was listening to a tape of my father singing opera. There was a big smile on her face as she listened. Why shouldn't she think the tape was lovely? She had a thick cotton hat covering her ears.

"Mom, why can't you be sick like other people?" I shouted above my father's off-key singing. "Take a pill! Watch TV! Sleep!"

"You'll see, I'll be better toborrow," she said. "By the way, please brig be by orange juice. It's tibe for be to gargle."

The next day, believe it or not, she was all better. She gave five fencing lessons and she ran around the house three times, singing along with the music in her radio earphones.

How could I get my mother to give up her weird sickness remedies if they worked?

Now that she was well, I decided to try something else. There was going to be a baked-goods and plant sale at the Town Hall to raise money for the Chesterville PTA. I figured that working at a PTA sale is a pretty normal thing for a mother to do. So I asked my mother if she wanted to sell cookies and plants at one of the tables.

She jumped at the chance. I wanted to help her

get ready for the sale, but she said she didn't need any help.

The day before the sale, she baked for hours. You've heard the expression, bake up a storm? Well, she baked up a hurricane. And all night, she was down in the basement, potting plants to sell.

I was glad to see her making such an effort for the PTA sale.

The next day, I rode my bike over to Town Hall to see how she was doing. It took me a while to get through the crowd that was gathered around her table. Then I saw what she was selling . . . She had giant cookies decorated like clocks, and breads shaped like elephants. She was also selling dandelion plants in flower pots.

While I was looking at my mother's table, someone tapped me on the shoulder. It was Roger Snooterman. I was not glad to see him.

"I helped set up the sale," Roger said. "If I had known your mother would be here, I would have made a special sign to say, 'Weirdo Table'."

I tried to ignore him, hoping he would go away.

But Roger had more to say. "Have you seen *my* mother's table?" he asked. "She's selling some beautiful roses. But you probably wouldn't be interested — she's not selling any weeds."

I could have kicked myself for not having insisted

that my mother let me help her decide what to sell.

Roger went back to his mother's table, and I listened to what the people at my mother's table were saying: "What imaginative cookies and breads! What *strange* cookies and breads! A dandelion for a house plant? I never realized how pretty dandelions are!"

At the end of the sale, the president of the PTA came over to my mother. I thought she would tell her to stick to plain chocolate-chip cookies and begonia plants next time. I figured that getting a lecture from the PTA president would teach my mother a lesson.

Instead, the PTA president thanked my mother for all her work. She said my mother's unusual table had made more money for the PTA than any other table at the sale.

"Next time, I'll make my fire engine cookies too," said my mother.

I was furious with the PTA. Here I was trying to get my mother to act normal, and the PTA president was thanking her for being weird.

Even though my mother was still weird, I decided to go ahead and work on my father. If I could get him to be normal, he could help me try to unweird my mother again.

The next Saturday, I asked my father to go with me to the library. The library was a perfect unweirding place, I figured. It would be a good place for him to practice being quiet, for one thing. And a father and daughter going to the library together was such a nice, normal activity. I could already hear myself saying to him after our successful day, "Isn't it fun to act normal, Daddy?"

He said he would be glad to go with me to the library. He even agreed to walk instead of riding his umbrella bicycle.

Sarah wanted to go with us and get out a book on sea urchins. I told her I would buy her two cans of mixed vegetables for her label collection if she stayed home. She said it was a deal.

There was an exhibit of Navaho dolls at the Chesterville Public Library. My father and I walked around and looked at the exhibit. He was nice and quiet. He whispered about which dolls he liked best.

A couple of the dolls were not in glass cases. My father started touching the beads on the dolls' dresses.

"Dad! Stop it!" I whispered.

"It's wonderful to touch things," he said. "Experience how smooth the beads are."

"You're not supposed to touch things in an exhibit," I said. "If everybody handled the dolls, they would get wrecked and fall apart."

"Of course, you're right," he said. And he didn't touch anything else in the exhibit. I was very pleased that he had listened to me. It seemed that he just needed to be alone with someone normal like me to learn how to behave. If weirdos like my mother and Sarah were around him all the time, how could he get normal?

After we saw the whole doll exhibit, we went to the children's library. My Young Blue Jay group was planning a field trip to a fish hatchery, so we found a big book with lots of pictures of fish. We looked through it together. My father spoke in whispers. He seemed to enjoy acting like a normal person in a library.

I was about to congratulate him on his behavior when a bunch of little kids came in for story hour. They sat down on the floor around the children's librarian.

The librarian began to read them the story of "Little Red Riding Hood." After she read each page, she held up the book to show them the pictures. Some of the kids weren't listening. They were squirming around and whispering.

My father was not pleased. "That librarian makes the story so dull," he whispered to me. "She reads with no expression."

"Look at this catfish," I said, pointing to a picture

in the fish book. I wanted to get his mind off the dull story hour. I didn't like the look in his eyes.

"So Little Red Riding Hood filled the picnic basket with goodies to take to her grandmother," the librarian was saying. "Pay attention, Robbie and Stevie!"

My father jumped out of his chair and went over to the story-hour group. "If you have no objection," he said, "I'll help make the story a little more interesting."

"Well . . ." the librarian started to say.

My father interrupted her: "Don't let me interrupt you — go right on reading."

The librarian started reading again in her soft, dull voice. And my father acted out the story. Whenever Little Red Riding Hood was mentioned, he walked around on his knees, smiling. When the story talked about the wolf, he walked on all fours and made a mean face.

Robbie and Stevie stopped squirming around and whispering. None of the other little kids fooled around anymore either. They were too busy listening to the story and watching the crazy man with long black hair hanging down from his bald head.

The parents waiting to take their kids home stared at my father too. He was jumping around, acting all the parts out. He was Little Red Riding Hood walk-

ing through the woods. He was the wolf hiding behind trees and pretending to be the grandmother in
bed. He was the woodsman running after the wolf
with an axe.

At the end of the story, the little kids cheered.
"Can you come to story hour again, Mister?" one
of them asked.

"It's a possibility," said my father.

The librarian frowned at him and put the "Little
Red Riding Hood" book back on the shelf.

"Let's go home," I whispered to my father.

"Wait!" he said. "I want to ask the librarian when
the next story hour will be."

I never knew how strong I was until then. I took
my father's hand and just about dragged him out of
the library.

"I guess you really wanted to leave," said my
father when we were outside. "I had a good time in
the library. Did you notice how quiet I was? I whispered the whole time, and while I acted out 'Little
Red Riding Hood,' I didn't say a word!"

I hardly said a word either while we walked home.
I didn't feel like talking to the Story Hour King.
Besides, I was already trying to think of a way to
unweird Sarah.

Maybe my parents were too old and set in their
ways to be unweirded first. But Sarah was young. If

I could get *her* to be normal, we could be an un-weirding team and work on our parents together.

Before we went home, my father and I bought the two cans of mixed vegetables I had promised Sarah for her label collection.

6

Blankets and Pizza on a Cold Summer Night

I waitcd for a chance to be alone in the house with Sarah to begin unweirding her. My plan was to get her to try all kinds of normal activities. When she found out how much fun it was to do normal things, she might give up her label collection, her dictionary reading, and her other weird interests. Maybe she would even trade Gomer for a dog.

I didn't have to wait long to be alone with Sarah. One night in August, our parents decided to go out for one of their backwards dinners.

"Where are you going to eat?" Sarah asked them.

"We're going to treat ourselves to everything from dessert to appetizers," my father said. "First, we're going to Cone Town for ice cream. Then we'll get a pear pie at Sally's Bakery. After that, we're going to Burger World for hamburgers. Then on to the

Soup Kettle for soup and salad. And finally, we'll stop at the Dockside Restaurant for shrimp cocktails."

"Have fun!" Sarah and I told them.

For some reason, Sarah and I get along best when our parents aren't home. When they left, she asked me, "What do you want to do?"

I suggested an activity that would make our house look more normal. "Let's prune the jungle," I said. And that's what we did.

The jungle is in our kitchen. Every time someone in my family eats a fruit or vegetable, we plant its seeds in one of the kitchen window boxes. We have grapefruit, avocado, peach, tomato, pepper, and pineapple plants and lots of others. We have just about every kind of fruit and vegetable plant you could think of (except broccoli) all tangled up in the kitchen jungle.

Sarah started pruning the plants in the window boxes on the left side of the kitchen and I pruned the ones on the right. By the time we met in the middle, the plants looked much better. It looked almost like a normal, unjungle kitchen.

Then I asked Sarah, "How would you like to bake?"

"Sure," she said. She was being so reasonable! She was even willing to try something normal, like baking.

We decided to bake a cake. I was afraid I would have to talk her out of baking it in some weird shape, but she got out a regular, round cake pan. Then we got out flour and eggs and butter and baking soda and salt and milk and vanilla. We mixed them all together.

But we couldn't find any sugar. We couldn't find any honey or molasses either.

"I know!" said Sarah. She went in her room and came back with two chocolate bars she had been saving since the last Halloween. We crumbled them up and added the chocolate crumbs to the batter.

After we got the cake in the oven, Patti dropped by. The kitchen was a real mess. We had sifted more flour onto the floor than into the bowl. There was batter all over the kitchen — on the refrigerator, the table, the oven door, the plants, the grand piano, and even in Sarah's bright red hair. I hadn't noticed the mess until Patti came over.

I said something to Patti that I heard a soap opera character say on one of Patti's TVs. I said, "What must you think of us? The place is a disgrace."

Patti made me feel better. "It's cool city," she said. "Creative cooks are always messy."

"I like the way your bangs are cut," Sarah said to Patti. "Your hair is such a beautiful blonde." Sarah was actually being polite! She talked for a while about how much homework she gets in the seventh grade and which teachers are O.K. and which aren't.

Then Patti said she had to go home. "My parents eat dinner at exactly six o'clock every night," she said. "They're dull city."

I thought how nice it would be to have a dull, normal family like Patti's. Maybe I *would* have one someday — either I would finally unweird my family or I would move in with hers.

When Patti left, Sarah took the cake out of the oven and cut it into pieces. We were pretty hungry, and we could hardly wait to eat. The cake smelled a little funny . . .

Sarah and I tasted the cake we had made. It was horrible! It didn't even taste like food. Did you ever eat a rubber eraser? I didn't either, but I think that cake tasted like one.

We spit out the bites we had taken, and we drank lots of water to wash away the taste. Then we opened the windows to air out the kitchen.

"I guess that leftover Halloween candy wasn't such a good idea," said Sarah. I was pleased to hear her admit she had made a mistake. "I'm starved," she said.

I tried to think of a normal dinner for two sisters to eat when their parents were out. "Let's order a pizza," I said.

Sarah called up the Chesterville House of Pizza. She ordered a large pizza because we were so hun-

gry. She ordered plain cheese on my half. On her half, she ordered chicken salad and sliced eggs. The pizza man made her give her order twice because he didn't believe it the first time.

I couldn't unweird her eating habits in just one night, I figured.

While we waited for the pizza, we tried to feed Gomer a piece of the cake. One good thing about sea urchins is that they eat just about anything. But even Gomer didn't seem to want our cake.

"You stubborn urchin," Sarah said to him.

"Wouldn't you rather have a dog for a pet?" I asked Sarah.

"If Gomer keeps being such a picky eater, I will," said Sarah.

I was hopeful.

Since Gomer wasn't interested in the cake, we cut it into little pieces and put them outside in some of our father's coconut-and-beer-can birdfeeders. Maybe birds don't have taste buds.

We noticed that it was very cold for August. It couldn't have been more than 50 degrees.

Soon after we went back inside, we heard the doorbell ring the first seven notes of "Somewhere Over the Rainbow."

"Who desires entrance and what is your purpose?" Sarah asked.

"Pizza man, pizza delivery," a man's voice said.

Sarah opened the door, and the pizza man handed her the pizza. "I was just listening to the news on the radio," he said. "This is the coldest August temperature in seventy-five years!"

"Wow!" Sarah said. We were all set to eat the pizza when the pizza man reminded us it wasn't free.

I didn't have any money! Sarah didn't have any money! Sarah handed the pizza back to the pizza man, and we went through the house on a money hunt.

The pizza man sat down on one of the living room mattresses and waited.

We looked for money everywhere. We looked in drawers, in cabinets, and under mattresses.

"I found them!" Sarah screamed.

I ran into her room to see how much money she had found. But it turned out she had found her six missing creamed corn labels. They were under her bed.

I peeked in at the pizza man. He had fallen asleep on a living room mattress with the pizza box on his stomach.

Sarah and I searched the whole house, but we just couldn't find any money. Even the gumball machine was out of pennies.

I felt like such a weirdo to have ordered pizza without having money.

We woke up the pizza man. "I'm sorry, we can't find any money," Sarah told him.

The pizza man was pretty mad. "I'm tired of kids ordering pizzas delivered to a phony address or not having money to pay," he said.

"I'm afraid you'll just have to take the pizza back," Sarah said.

"What good will that do?" said the pizza man. "No one else is going to want pizza with chicken salad and sliced eggs on half of it."

"We'll have to pay you later then," said Sarah.

"You *better* pay me later!" the pizza man said. "Get the money to me by eight o'clock tonight or I'll . . . I'll call the police."

He shoved the pizza box into Sarah's hands. There was a huge grease circle on his stomach where the pizza box had been lying. He stomped out the door, muttering, "Crazy kids — chicken-salad-and-sliced-egg pizza . . ."

I DID NOT want the pizza man to call the police on us. I DID NOT want to borrow money from a neighbor either because I DID NOT want to have to explain why we needed it.

Sarah said she would come up with a way to pay the pizza man before eight o'clock. She put on Dad's safari hat to help her think.

I turned on the oven and put the pizza box in to keep it warm.

"I've got it!" Sarah said. She told me her money-making idea. It sounded kind of strange, but I didn't have time to worry about unweirding her then. I wanted to do something fast so we wouldn't get in trouble with the police . . .

We took all the blankets off Sarah's bed, my bed, and our parents' bed, and we took the extra blankets out of the hall closet. We folded them and put them into two plastic garbage bags. Then we each carried a bag over our shoulders and set off for the Chesterville Cinema.

It was almost time for the seven o'clock show of a new movie called *The Two-Hour Minute.*

There was a long line of people waiting to get in. You could tell that the people in the line were cold because a lot of them hopped from one leg to the other.

Sarah took roller skates out of her plastic garbage bag and started skating up and down the sidewalk next to the line. Her curly red hair shone brightly under the street lights. She shouted: "It's a cold night, folks! It's the coldest August evening in seventy-five years! Get your wool blankets here! Genuine wool blankets! Five dollars apiece!"

She took a blanket out of her bag and held it up for the crowd to see. "Doesn't that look warm?" she asked. She put it over her shoulders and said, "That sure feels good."

"I'll take one," said a man wearing shorts and a short-sleeved shirt. He paid for the blanket and wrapped it around himself.

Then a teenage boy bought one, and he and his girlfriend both wore it like a giant shawl.

Sarah's plan was working out pretty well. Soon, she sold all the blankets in her bag. I gave her my plastic garbage bag, and she sold the rest of the blankets in about five minutes.

I was relieved that we had money to pay for our pizza, and we wouldn't get into trouble with the police. But then, I realized that we had sold all the blankets in the house and we had only needed to sell *one* to pay for the pizza!

I told Sarah we had sold all the blankets and we hadn't needed to.

"Now you tell me!" she said.

Sarah roller-skated and I walked to the pizza parlor. The pizza delivery man was working behind the counter.

"Here's the money," said Sarah. She gave him a five-dollar bill. I noticed that she still had a bunch of five-dollar bills left.

I wondered if weirdness might be contagious. It wasn't like me to go along with Sarah's crazy blanket-selling idea. When the pizza man threatened to call the police, I had forgotten all about my plan to unweird Sarah. Instead of my unweirding her, she seemed to be making *me* weird.

"Sorry you had to wait for the money," I said to the pizza man before we left.

"Well, don't let it happen again," he said.

He smiled at me. I could tell he felt sorry for me because I had a weirdo for a sister. He could probably tell that I was getting weird too. I also noticed that he still had the pizza-sized grease circle on his stomach.

Sarah and I went home.

When we opened the front door to our house, I knew something was wrong. The house smelled terrible, and the air was smoky.

I ran into the kitchen. Smoke was pouring out of the oven. I turned it off and opened the oven door. The pizza box was all black, and it was sending off smoke signals.

I knew my parents would be coming home any minute, and I was worried. The kitchen was still splattered with batter, the house smelled, the air was filled with smoke, and we had sold all the blankets in the house!

All Sarah said was: "I'm starved. It's too bad the pizza got all dried out." At least she didn't make a big deal about how I had left the oven on.

Just then, our parents came home. My mother started gargling with orange juice right away.

"Your mother has a slight case of indigestion from eating too much," my father said.

"I feel much better now," my mother said when she finished gargling. "Isn't it kind of smoky in here?"

"Oh, Mom, I'm so sorry," I said. "I left the oven on and burned the pizza box. And we didn't have any money to pay for the pizza, so we sold the blankets and . . ."

"What? Slow down," my father said.

"It's all very logical," said Sarah. And she told them the story of our evening.

Suddenly, we heard a siren. It got louder and louder. Finally, it stopped, and the "Somewhere Over the Rainbow" doorbell rang.

"Who could that be?" my mother said.

We all went to the door. There were two firemen. One held a hose and one held an axe. "Where's the fire?" the one with the hose shouted as he rushed into the living room.

"Oh, there's no fire," my father said.

"Someone riding by, I think Snooterman was his name, reported smoke coming out of your kitchen window," the fireman with the axe said. "It sure smells like smoke in here!"

"Everything is under control now," said my mother. "You see, the kids ordered this chicken-salad-and-sliced-egg pizza . . ."

Why does my mother have to be so honest? She told the firemen every detail of our weird evening, from the pizza to the blankets to the fact that she was planning to keep a ten-dollar bill in the encyclopedia under "money" in case we needed cash in a hurry again.

The firemen kept looking at each other and rolling their eyes. By the end of the story, they were sitting down on mattresses because they were tired of standing there listening.

"Well, young lady," the one with the axe said to me. "I guess you know now not to do something weird like leave pizza in a cardboard box in the oven."

Since we had wasted the firemen's time, my mother signed them up for ten free fencing lessons each.

After they left, I apologized to my parents for the trouble I had caused.

"There's nothing to be sorry for," said my mother. "I'm sure you learned your lesson about leaving a box in the oven. And I think you were very clever to think of a way to make money."

"Yes, you were very imaginative," said my father.

"You're not angry with us for selling all the blankets?" I asked.

"Of course not," said my father. "I know how it is to get carried away once in a while. We'll just use sleeping bags tonight, and we'll buy new blankets tomorrow. The leftover money you made by selling all the old blankets should buy one or two new ones."

"What about the mess in the kitchen?" I asked.

"We'll all clean it up either tonight or tomorrow," said my mother. "I'm just glad you didn't start a serious fire, and I'm glad you girls had fun."

I had to admit to myself that I actually did have fun with Sarah part of the time.

Sarah gave Gomer a piece of the dried-out pizza. He must have liked it because it disappeared in a couple of minutes. "That reminds me," Sarah said, "I'm starved."

"Me too," I said.

Luckily, my parents had gotten so full after the first five courses of their backwards dinner that they couldn't eat their appetizers. So Sarah and I had a delicious meal of leftover stuffed clams and shrimp cocktails. I wondered if there were some advantages to having weirdos for parents.

I started thinking that a lot of parents would yell if you sold all the blankets. And they might send you to your room if you left the house all dirty and smoky. One good thing about having weird parents is that they don't mind if *you* do something weird.

That's when it hit me — I was definitely getting weird too. Even the fireman had said that leaving a pizza box in the oven was weird.

My one-at-a-time unweirding plan hadn't worked with my mother, my father, *or* my sister. It was just a matter of time before I got as weird as the rest of my family. That night, I had ordered a pizza without having money to pay for it. I had helped Sarah sell all our blankets, and I had almost started a fire. The next day, I might be twirling a baton on a skateboard and collecting different color shoelaces!

Maybe I should move in with Patti before it's too late, I thought.

7

An Evening With Unweirdos

Patti suggested that I spend an evening at her house to see if I really liked it there. I was planning to move in with her if it turned out there was no hope of unweirding my family or staying normal myself.

Not long after school started, Patti invited me over for dinner. She and I are in different fifth-grade classes this year. I'm in Mrs. Reed's class again. (Mrs. Reed moved up to fifth grade from fourth grade, like me.) Patti is in Mr. Howard's fifth-grade class.

All day, I looked forward to spending an evening with unweirdos. School was horrible that day. Mrs. Reed told us to write a composition about an activity we had done with our families over the weekend.

There's nothing I hate more than assignments like "What I Did Over the Weekend" or "My Summer

Vacation." I can never think of anything good to write about because everything my family does is weird. I could call my compositions "What the Weirdos Did on Vacation" or "Help, I'm a Prisoner in a Weird Family."

I thought about everything we had done over the weekend — from transplanting weeds to playing the pretend orchestra game to having an open house for my mother's fencing students. Everything was too weird to write about.

Finally, I decided to write about painting on the living room wall. My family had painted a new mural to get ready for the open house. I didn't have anything else better to do, so I painted too.

We used white paint to cover the mural we had painted with Marguerite. When the white paint dried, we painted a mural of our favorite foods. Sarah painted a chicken-salad-and-sliced-egg pizza. My mother painted her dream — a drinking fountain that spouted orange juice. My father painted *his* favorite, burnt toast. I painted a hamburger and french fries.

I DID NOT realize that Mrs. Reed would make us read our compositions out loud. She had never done anything like that the year before. She used to be so nice!

When we finished writing, Mrs. Reed said: "Now we will share some of our compositions with each other. It will be good practice for you to read out loud. And it will help you get to know each other, since you weren't all in the same class last year."

If I had known about the sharing with the class stuff, I wouldn't have written about something like painting on the living room wall. I would have written that my family watched a baseball game on TV.

I sat in my seat, thinking, *Don't call on me, don't call on me.*

"Cindy, how about you?" asked Mrs. Reed.

I was ready for her. I pointed at my throat and whispered, "Sorry, Mrs. Reed. I have laryngitis." I hoped I looked pale and sick. Judging by the way my face felt, though, it was probably red. Maybe she thought I was flushed with a fever.

"I'm sorry to hear that you're sick," Mrs. Reed said.

It worked! I thought.

"Since you have laryngitis," said Mrs. Reed, "I'll read your composition to the class for you."

There was no way out. I handed her my composition without looking her in the eye. She read it out loud while I stared at people's feet. Everybody in my class heard about my family's habit of painting on the living room wall.

When Mrs. Reed finished, Brenda, who was in my class three years in a row, said, "That's the strangest thing I ever heard! Who paints on their wall?"

"I've seen Cindy's family's living room murals and they're beautiful," said Grant. "I wish my family would do stuff like that."

"Me too!" said a girl named Molly.

Grant and Molly probably said those things to make me feel better, I figured. It didn't work.

After that, other kids read compositions about normal things their families had done over the weekend. Brenda read about going bowling. Karen Berman wrote about visiting a whaling museum. Seth Andrews actually *volunteered* to read his composition. He and his family had gone to his cousin's wedding in New Jersey, and he got to stay up until midnight.

During lunch, Grant told me he was glad Mrs. Reed hadn't called on him.

"Why?" I asked.

"My family did something really embarrassing over the weekend. And it was all I could think of to write about."

I didn't bug him to tell me what his family had done, but I was dying to know.

"I'll tell you if you promise not to tell anyone," Grant said.

"I promise," I said.

"Well," said Grant, "my father's boss came over for dinner, and my parents were really nervous about it. My mother spilled coffee on the boss's jacket by mistake. My father was so busy trying to clean the jacket that he forgot he was running water for my little brother's bath. It overflowed and started a flood all the way into the living room!"

"What a mess!" I said.

Grant's weekend sounded embarrassing all right, but not half as embarrassing as most of my weekends were.

I wasn't in the mood for being embarrassed any more than necessary that night at Patti's. I wanted her parents to like me enough to want me to move in.

I went to Patti's house at exactly six o'clock, because that's when her family always eats. They said hello to me, and we sat down at the table. Patti's parents had to sit kind of far from the table because they have big stomachs. You can tell they don't ride bikes to work or jog around the house. You can tell that Patti's father has someone else carry his golf clubs when he plays golf.

Everybody got their own plate, not like in my house, where everybody eats dinner out of one pot.

Patti's father turned on the color TV in the kitchen. (There's another color TV in the den and a black-and-white set in the master bedroom.) I was surprised that they watched TV during dinner. Usually, I go to Patti's right after school and I go home at dinnertime.

The news was on.

We each ate half a grapefruit. I tried to be very careful so I wouldn't squirt anyone.

Everybody was really quiet. I thought her parents might be thinking about Marguerite's article in the *Chesterville News*. Or maybe Roger Snooterman had told them stories about my family when he delivered the paper. Maybe they just didn't feel like talking to a kid from a weirdo family.

I figured I should start a conversation to show them I wasn't so bad. I said, "This grapefruit is delicious!"

"Ssh," Patti's father said. He didn't seem to want to have anything to do with me. I figured that he was probably angry with Patti for inviting me for dinner in the first place. And she had said they wouldn't mind if I moved in!

When a commercial came on, Patti's father asked, "How do you like being in the Young Blue Jays, Cindy?"

I told him I liked it and that my group went on a field trip to a fish hatchery.

"That's nice," Patti's mother said.

When the commercial was over, everybody got quiet again. I started to catch on that they only talked during commercials.

When the next commercial came on, Patti's father told me about a fish hatchery he had visited once. During the commercial after that, Patti's mother said that fish had gotten very expensive.

I had never eaten any of the foods we had for dinner before, except grapefruit. Patti's mother served fried chicken she had bought frozen in a box, peas and corn out of a can, and pound cake from a box. Everything was delicious!

I thought it would be nice to know that dinner would always be ready at exactly six o'clock. The only thing my family did at the same time every night was scream, at nine o'clock.

I also thought it would be nice to eat from my very own plate at dinner, and to know that I only had to talk during commercials. I thought it would be nice to live with an ordinary family that I wouldn't have to feel embarrassed by.

After dinner, we cleaned up the kitchen. Then Patti's parents watched the color TV in the den, and Patti and I talked in her room. She has a big room for such a short person. It used to be her sister's room before her sister got married. The smaller bedroom used to be Patti's. That would be my room if I moved in.

"I bet it's nice to live in a normal household," I said.

"It's really dull city sometimes," said Patti.

"Everything is always the same. Dinner at six, TV every night. Every Friday, my mother goes to the hairdresser. Every Saturday, my father plays golf or watches golf on TV."

"I would like all that," I said. "I'm tired of weird surprises."

"Things were a little livelier when my big sister was still here," Patti said. "At least, she used to pick on me, and we would fight once in a while."

"I don't think I would miss fighting with Sarah," I said.

"It's too bad you don't realize how great your family is," Patti said. "But if you're really unhappy, I can talk to my parents about your moving in."

"Well . . ." I said.

Just then, we heard the doorbell ring. It didn't play any tunes, like the doorbell at my house. It just went "ding dong."

"Patti!" her father called. "Your Aunt Luba is here. Come bring your tap shoes."

"Sugar!" Patti muttered. "Sugar, salt, and pepper!"

"Come on, Patti!" her father called.

"Dad, I don't feel like it," Patti said.

"I'll give you two minutes to get into the living room," her father announced.

Patti took a pair of tap shoes out of her closet and put them on.

"I didn't know you knew how to tap-dance," I said.

"Well now you know," Patti said.

"How did you learn?" I asked.

"My parents make me take lessons," she said. "I hate it."

I followed her into the living room. Her mother put on a record called "Tap Favorites." Then Patti's mother and father and Aunt Luba sat on the couch. All three of them were pretty fat, and they kept their hands folded on their stomach.

Patti stood on the flagstones in front of the fireplace until "East Side, West Side" started playing. Then she started dancing. Her short blonde hair bounced up and down while she tap-danced. She danced really well, and the taps sounded great on the flagstones. But you could tell she hated it.

"Smile, Patti!" Aunt Luba said. So Patti danced with this phony-looking smile that had a frown underneath.

Afterwards, everyone clapped. Patti kissed Aunt Luba, and we went back to her room. She took off her tap shoes and threw them into the back of her closet.

"You were super," I said.

"Too bad," said Patti. "If they didn't think I had any talent, they would let me quit."

"Why do your parents make you take lessons if you don't like them?" I asked.

"Because my father always wanted to take lessons when *he* was a kid," Patti said. "But he couldn't afford them."

"What does that have to do with you?" I asked.

Patti shrugged. "The worst part is they make me dance whenever relatives come over," she said. "It's so embarrassing!"

Patti didn't feel much like talking anymore. So I thanked her parents for dinner and walked back to my house.

I did a lot of thinking on my way home. I was surprised to find out that Patti's normal, totally unweird parents were embarrassing too. Maybe moving in with them wasn't the answer.

I remembered that Grant's parents were embarrassing too, over the last weekend anyway.

It seemed that my family wasn't the only embarrassing one around. At least they didn't make me tap-dance in front of relatives. They didn't yell at me for selling all our blankets and almost starting a fire either.

When I got home, my parents and Sarah were in the middle of their nightly screaming session. I went outside and waited until it was over.

Maybe other people had embarrassing families too. But, after hearing the screaming session, I was still sure *no one's* family could be as embarrassing as mine. I was tired of their weird behavior. I was tired of their screaming together every night. I was tired of only having weird things to write about in compositions at school and hiding in the closet when Roger Snooterman delivered the paper.

I decided to try one last unweirding plan. I promised myself that it would be my last try. If that didn't work . . . well . . . I didn't want to move in with Patti anymore . . . so it just *had* to work!

8

One Last Chance

I was sure my last unweirding plan was foolproof. The regular leader of my Young Blue Jay group was on vacation. So I asked my parents if they wanted to take the group on a hike. They said they would be glad to. Sarah said she would come too.

I had told my family so much about the Young Blue Jays that I was sure they would know how to act around them. Just to make sure, I had everyone in my family read the Young Blue Jay Handbook. That way, they would be sure to know all the rules and nothing could go wrong, I figured. They would have so much fun being normal, for a change, that they would volunteer to unweird themselves forever after! I looked forward to being able to look Roger Snooterman in the eye again.

If my plan backfired, and Sarah and my parents acted weird even with all my preparation, all the

Young Blue Jays would find out I had a weird family. They might even throw me out of the group. But it was a chance I had to take if I was ever going to unweird my family.

The day of the hike, I asked my mother if she would try to act normal all day, while the Young Blue Jays were around.

"Who?" she asked.

"The Young Blue Jays!" I said. "Our hike is to-day!"

"Oh, that's right," she said.

"Well, will you?" I asked.

"Will I what?" she answered.

"Will you act normal?" I asked.

"Of course, Cindy," she said. "I'll act the same as always."

That's just what I was afraid of.

My stomach felt like a whole lot of bumblebees were in it. While Sarah and my parents got dressed, I went into the kitchen and played the piano to calm myself down.

Then I heard the doorbell ring the first seven notes of "Somewhere Over the Rainbow."

I opened the door.

"What a funny doorbell," one of the Young Blue Jays said. The bees in my stomach started buzzing around even more.

The Blue Jays came in and looked around. There

were eight of them. There was only one of me.

It was the first time my Young Blue Jay group had been in my house. They pointed things out to each other — the gumball machine, the living room mural of different foods, my father's indoor exercise bicycle, the jungle in our kitchen — I wished we had arranged to meet at the Tulip Mountain parking lot instead of at our house. I also wished that Patti was in the Young Blue Jays instead of the Young Raccoons.

"What's this?" asked one of the Blue Jays.

"That's Gomer, our pet sea urchin," I mumbled.

Then Sarah came into the living room. She was wearing her karate suit for the hike. And, of course, she had her baton.

"Hi, Sarah," said one of the Blue Jays who lives in our neighborhood.

Sarah didn't answer. She fed Gomer some leftover split-pea soup she had eaten for breakfast.

"Hi, Sarah," another Blue Jay said. But Sarah still didn't answer.

"Sarah!" I said.

Finally, Sarah turned to the Blue Jays. She announced: "My name is not Sarah. I have changed my name to Ethel."

"Since when?" I asked.

"Since this morning," she said. She looked really proud of herself. I started to wish she would stay home and read the D's in the dictionary instead of going on the hike with us.

I found my mother wrapping sandwiches in the kitchen. At least, she remembered to bring lunch. "Mom, why did you let Sarah change her name to Ethel?" I asked.

"Why not?" she answered.

"I think it's just awful," I said. "It's weird to change your name, especially to Ethel."

"Whatever she wants to be called is O.K. with me," my mother said. "I changed *my* name from Crystal to Squirrel, you know."

"Sarah's only a child," I said. "She's too young to change her name. "How would you like it if I changed *my* name to . . . to . . . Caboose?" I asked.

"That would be fine with me," my mother said.

There was no use talking to her. I stomped out of the kitchen.

My father was in the living room with the Blue Jays. He was explaining how he had painted his watercolor tattoos. He had one of a butterfly and one of an apple that day.

"I'd like to try painting tattoos some time," said one of the Young Blue Jays.

When everybody was ready, we piled into the rainbow van. My father rode next to us on his bicycle. He rode with the umbrella open because it was sunny.

At the center of Chesterville, there was a policeman directing traffic. My father beeped the first four notes of "Frère Jacques" on his bicycle horn. The policeman jumped about six inches.

"Just saying hello," my father shouted. He tipped his safari hat at the policeman.

The Blue Jays laughed and said, "Did you see the cop jump?" I didn't think it was funny at all. I thought you could even get arrested for scaring a policeman. Luckily, the policeman just smiled and shook his finger at my father.

We drove to the Tulip Mountain parking lot and parked near the beginning of a trail. My father locked his bike to a tree, and we started hiking.

Sarah (or rather, Ethel) twirled her baton while she walked. My father picked dandelions and made necklaces out of them for all the Blue Jays. I threw mine away. I wasn't interested in his weeds.

After a while, we came to a level spot, and we stopped for lunch. My mother unpacked the food. She had brought orange juice and inside-out peanut-butter-and-jelly sandwiches — in air-sickness bags, of course.

Did you ever try to eat a peanut-butter-and-jelly sandwich with the bread on the inside? At least my mother brought lots of napkins.

Sarah (or rather, Ethel) didn't eat a peanut-butter-and-jelly sandwich. She is the only person in the

world who doesn't like jelly. She ate a peanut-butter-and-cucumber sandwich instead.

One of the Young Blue Jays had brought along a Young Blue Jay Handbook. She asked my father why he was wearing short sleeves. The handbook says you should wear long sleeves on hikes so you won't get insect bites.

"I have my own methods," said my father. "Before we left, I rubbed my arms with pickle juice to keep the bugs away. That was before I painted on the tattoos, of course."

The Blue Jays giggled. They probably thought he was kidding.

The Blue Jay with the handbook asked my mother why she was wearing sneakers. The handbook says you're supposed to wear sturdy shoes on hikes.

"Why, I'd go crazy without my red sneakers," said my mother. She looked pretty crazy as it was, with her wild-looking gray hair, a pink warm-up suit, and red sneakers.

Of course, Ethel had to start talking about her dumb can label collection. "I have two hundred seventy-four creamed corn labels in my room," she said.

"No kidding!" said one of the Blue Jays.

"Wow!" another Blue Jay said.

They were trying to be polite. The Young Blue Jay

Handbook says you should always be polite. The Blue Jays also told my mother the lunch was delicious.

We rested for a while. Then we started climbing again.

"I asked *my* parents to take our group on a hike," said one of the Blue Jays. "My mother said she had to play bridge, and my father said he had to take it easy on Saturdays because he works hard all week."

"I asked my parents to take us too," another Blue Jay said. "But they were going to a wedding."

I was starting to wish my parents had been too busy to take us.

When we got to another clearing, we took a rest break. "Do you want to hear my bird imitations?" asked my mother.

Before anyone answered, she climbed a tree. My father followed her. They sat on a branch and did bird calls.

The Blue Jays cheered. Maybe I would have cheered too if they weren't my parents. But they were.

It didn't take long to climb the last part of the trail. Suddenly, we were at a clearing on top of the mountain.

"We made it!" the Blue Jays said.

The view was something else. We could see way

down into the valley. We could see houses in Chesterville and cars driving along roads. Everything looked so small.

Naturally, my family couldn't act like normal people on a hike and just say, "What a nice view!"

Ethel twirled her baton and did a victory cheer. She made up the words: "Mommy drove us, Daddy biked. Then up, up, up we hiked. Who are the greatest hikers today? We all know, it's the Young Blue Jays!"

My mother did cartwheels. My father sang a song from an Italian opera. He leaned his head back and looked up at the sky while he sang. That made his safari hat fall off, and you could see the bald top of his head. It wouldn't have been quite as embarrassing if he could sing on key.

I couldn't take it anymore. I walked away to be by myself.

I walked until I could hardly hear the opera singing. Then I sat under a tree.

I felt miserable.

My family was ruining the Young Blue Jay hike with their weird behavior. The Young Blue Jays were too polite to show they were miserable too, but I was sure they were. They would probably ask me to leave the group, and I wouldn't blame them if they did.

I was sure the Blue Jays would be too polite to

come right out and say that I had to leave because my family was weird. Maybe they would say that I had to leave because the Blue Jay Handbook says to be quiet in the woods, and my family had made more noise than a rocket taking off for the moon.

I was very disappointed that my unweirding plan wasn't working. And this was my family's last chance!

Suddenly, I noticed that the opera singing had stopped. And there were no cheers, no whoops, no bird calls . . . I walked back to where everyone had been. There was no one there. I looked in every corner of the clearing at the top of the mountain. Then I realized that everyone must have gone down the mountain without me.

I was all by myself on top of the mountain.

I felt very scared.

9

Weirdos to the Rescue

Maybe I can still catch up with them, I thought.

I tried to figure out which trail my family and the Blue Jays had taken down the mountain. There were five different trails, and they might have chosen any one of them.

I walked on the beginning of each trail and yelled, "Mommee! Daddee! Blue Jays!" But there was no answer.

My father once told me that if I got lost, I should go to the lost and found department or stay in one place and wait. There was no lost and found department on the mountain. There was no lifeguard with a bullhorn either. So I sat on a rock and waited.

I could tell that it would be dark in about an hour. If my parents didn't notice I was missing until they got home, they wouldn't even *start* looking for me until it was dark. I hate the dark. I even sleep with a night light. Now, I didn't have a night light with me. And even if I did, there was no place on top of Tulip Mountain to plug it in.

I wondered if there were grizzly bears living on the mountain. I wondered if there were bats.

I once saw a really scary movie about bats. They came after these kids who were trapped in a cave. I kept thinking about those bats while I waited on the rock to be rescued. Then I heard someone scream. "Eek!" It was me.

Don't think about the bats, I thought.

It was really quiet on the mountain. It was too quiet. I could hear every leaf move and every bird peep. Every leaf moving sounded like a grizzly bear. Every bird flying by reminded me of a bat.

I noticed that the wind was getting stronger. All I had over my shirt was a thin jacket. It can get cold on top of mountains at night. I DID NOT want to die of exposure. The Blue Jay Handbook didn't say anything about what to do if you were alone and scared and cold on top of a mountain.

Think of something pleasant, I told myself.

I thought how happy I would be when my parents showed up. They just *had* to show up.

Then I remembered that it would be weirdos who were coming to my rescue. Even if I were rescued, I would still have to face the Young Blue Jays. Nothing good was in store for me at the bottom of the mountain — only getting kicked out of the Blue Jays and more embarrassment. I was afraid of what would happen to me on top of the mountain and afraid of what would happen on the bottom.

Suddenly, I heard leaves rustling very loudly. I looked where the rustle had come from and I saw . . . a skunk.

The skunk stopped moving when it saw me. It stared at me. I stared at it.

Please don't spray me, I thought.

I knew that skunks spray when they're frightened. So I tried to look friendly. I smiled at the skunk to show it how friendly I was. I sat very still so it wouldn't think I would hurt it or anything. It didn't smile back.

This is just terrific, I thought. There I was, alone on top of a mountain — cold, scared, embarrassed. And then that dumb skunk had to bother me too. Roger Snooterman would probably have laughed himself silly just to see me sitting on a rock, smiling at a skunk.

I was worried enough that people wouldn't like me because I had a weird family. Now I was also worried that people would start calling me Skunky if I got sprayed.

Grant's dog once got sprayed by a skunk. After a

whole week and fourteen tomato-juice baths, he still smelled like a skunk.

I remembered hearing that animals think you're going to attack if you stare at them. So I stopped smiling at the skunk. I stopped looking at it altogether. I curled up on a rock and closed my eyes. I hoped the skunk would figure I was asleep and go away.

Then I heard leaves rustling again. *Oh, please don't spray me,* I thought.

I lay curled up on the rock for ages, pretending to be asleep. Every once in a while, I heard the skunk.

The rock felt cold and hard through my thin shirt and jacket. When would my parents show up? Even if they did show up, I thought sadly, they probably wouldn't notice the skunk. They would scare it by mistake and get all of us sprayed.

After ages and ages, I decided no one was coming, not before dark anyway. But I could still hear the skunk moving around, so I kept lying on the rock, pretending to be asleep. *Please don't spray me, skunk,* I kept thinking. *Please come rescue me, Mommy and Daddy.*

After what seemed like hours, I heard the rustling come closer. And closer! Then something wet was on my cheek. My heart pounded. "Aach!" I screamed.

I opened my eyes, and there was my mother!

"Take it easy," she said. She gave me one of her bear hugs and another kiss. "You sure woke up on the wrong side of the rock," she said.

"Woke up?" I said. "I wasn't sleeping. I was trying to fool the — aach — did you see the skunk?"

"We sure did," my mother said. "Your father and I got it to leave."

"How?" I asked. My heart was still pounding about a thousand times a minute.

"Well, we brought some popcorn along in case you were hungry when we found you," my mother explained. "Ethel and the Young Blue Jays made it in the picnic area at the bottom of the mountain. We first noticed you were missing when we couldn't find you in the picnic area to give you some popcorn. Anyway, when your father and I saw the skunk, we were very quiet, and we made a trail of popcorn leading from the skunk into the woods. The skunk ate the trail and disappeared!"

Just then, my father came out of the woods and said, "The skunk is gone now. I'm so glad to see you, Cindy!" He picked me up and twirled me around.

"I am too," said my mother. She did a cartwheel.

"I'm sure glad to see both of you," I said. I was so relieved that I wouldn't have to spend the night on the mountain with a skunk that I started to cry. It's funny, but sometimes you cry when you're happy.

My parents started to cry too when they saw me crying. They came over to me, and the three of us hugged. We made kind of a hug sandwich.

In the middle of the hug sandwich, I remembered how much I loved my parents. Maybe they were weird, but they were the kindest people you'd ever want to meet. They wouldn't even hurt a head of broccoli or a dandelion.

"I'm so sorry you got left behind," said my father.

"We thought you were with us," said my mother.

"I know you didn't leave me on purpose," I said. "It's my own fault for wandering off."

"Why did you?" asked my mother.

I didn't think it was a good time to tell them that I had wandered off because they're weird. They had just climbed a mountain twice and rescued me from a skunk. They were there when I needed them, just as they always were.

"I had some things to think about," I said.

I *still* had things to think about. As we walked down the mountain, I kept thinking about the Young Blue Jays waiting for me at the bottom. They were probably all set to kick me out of the group. Just because I was glad to see my parents didn't mean anyone else would appreciate them.

My father picked me up on his shoulders and gave me a ride down the mountain.

The closer we came to the bottom, the more nervous I got about seeing the Blue Jays. They would surely kick me out of the group. Not only was my family weird, but *I* had gone and wandered off like a weirdo.

By the time we reached the bottom of the mountain, it was getting dark. The trail ended in the picnic area, where Ethel and the Blue Jays were sitting around a campfire. They were all wearing the dandelion necklaces my father had made. Ethel was explaining the best way to take a label off a can.

As my father let me down off his shoulders, the bumblebees in my stomach buzzed around wildly. I waited for someone to tell me there was no room for weirdos in the Young Blue Jays.

But first, the Blue Jays and even Ethel wanted to hear all about my adventures on top of the mountain. I told them about being cold and scared. I told them about worrying about grizzly bears and bats and then meeting a skunk instead. Then I told them about how my parents got the skunk to leave.

I waited for them to tell me my days as a Blue Jay were over.

"Well, everything is O.K. now that you're back," one of the Blue Jays said.

Now that they know I'm safe, they'll break it to me that I ought to be in the Young Cuckoos instead of the Young Blue Jays, I thought.

"Cindy, you were a genius to ask your family to

take us on a hike!" said one of the Blue Jays. "This has been the best Blue Jays hike ever!"

"What?" I said. I couldn't believe my ears.

"This has been a really fantastic day," she said, "except that you got left behind, of course."

The Blue Jays all started talking at once: "It's been great! Yeah! I liked Mr. Krinkle's opera singing. I wish *my* mother could do cartwheels. I liked the way Mr. and Mrs. Krinkle do bird calls. They're such nice people too! I liked Sarah's — I mean — Ethel's baton twirling . . ."

I wasn't hearing things. The Young Blue Jays liked my family. They really liked my family! They weren't just being polite.

They couldn't stop talking about how much fun they had! "Those inside-out sandwiches were great. And don't you love these dandelion necklaces?"

Patti had been right all along. People thought my family was special, not just weird.

I felt pretty great hearing the Young Blue Jays rave about the hike with my family. And I realized something terrific — I wouldn't have to worry anymore about what Roger Snooterman or anyone else thought of me or my family. I wouldn't have to be embarrassed when my family did something embarrassing — because I wouldn't think it was embarrassing anymore. Maybe I could even enjoy my family again . . .

"We should get going," said my mother. "I can tell by my stomach that it's suppertime."

"Can't we stay just a little longer?" one of the Blue Jays asked. "Our parents know we might be home late."

"Let's play the pretend orchestra game," I said. "It's a game only my family plays," I told the Blue Jays.

"I guess we can stay and play for a little while," my mother said with a grin.

Ethel turned on the radio in the rainbow van, so we could hear orchestra music in the picnic area. She put some more wood on the campfire. I decided that even Ethel, or Sarah, or whatever her name was, had her good points.

I explained the pretend orchestra game to the Young Blue Jays. Then we started to play. We listened to the orchestra music and moved our hands and mouths as if we were playing different instruments. My mother pretended to play a tuba. My father pretended to play a bassoon. Ethel pretended to play a bass drum. The Blue Jays pretended to play violins, clarinets, and trumpets.

I borrowed Ethel's baton, and I pretended to be the conductor.

It was lots of fun. I felt proud to be part of such a weird, but terrific family.

10

Postscript: Trick or Treat with the Weirdos

Things went a lot better for me after the Young Blue Jay hike. It didn't unweird my family, but I found out that I didn't have to unweird them. Or even want to.

I didn't worry about what people thought of my family anymore, even though they *are* different from other people's families. Take Halloween, for instance. My family did a lot of stuff I *could* have been embarrassed by . . .

You should have seen the Halloween treats my mother gave out. She put them in air-sickness bags. She filled each bag with two pieces of bubble gum from our living room gumball machine, three of her home-baked fire engine cookies, and a paperback book. "Food for thought," she explained.

Sarah, who had changed her name back from Ethel, said: "Mom, you're not supposed to give out unwrapped cookies. I heard it on the radio. They tell kids not to eat anything that didn't come from a store, wrapped up."

So my mother wrote on each air-sickness bag: "No poison in here. Guaranteed delicious treats from Squirrel Krinkle, 75 Ash Street, Chesterville."

"That ought to do the trick," she said. "The trick for the treats!" She asked me if I wanted to eat dinner before or after I went trick-or-treating. I said I would rather eat later.

While my mother gave out treats to the little kids who came early, I got dressed. Patti and I were going trick-or-treating together.

I had made my own costume. I took an old gray shirt and old gray pants and painted little white boxes on them that were supposed to be windows. I took a paper bag and cut eye, nose, and mouth holes in it. Then I taped a long piece of wire to the top of the paper bag. The wire shot straight up into the air when I put the paper bag over my head. I wanted it to look like an antenna at the top of a building.

I put on my costume and went into the living room to wait for Patti. I was careful to keep my arms straight at my sides because buildings don't have arms.

"What are you supposed to be?" Sarah asked.

"The Empire State Building," I said.

Sarah groaned.

"I remember this house!" a little kid at the door said. "You gave out inside-out cheese sandwiches last Halloween."

When Patti showed up, she and I started giggling. We both looked so funny!

Patti was wearing a great costume. She had cardboard covered with wrapping paper all around her body. On top of her blonde head, she had a ribbon tied in a big bow. On the front of the cardboard, she had written, "Surprise!" She was a surprise package.

"Hey, nice package!" Sarah said. I knew she would compliment Patti's costume just to rub it in that she didn't think mine was so hot. I didn't care. It was Halloween. I love Halloween — *everybody* is weird on Halloween!

"Why don't you come trick-or-treating with us?" Patti asked Sarah.

It wouldn't have taken Sarah long to change. She always looks as if she's wearing a costume anyway. But she said, "I have more important things to do." She was probably going to clean Gomer's bowl.

Patti and I were just about to leave when someone wearing a white airplane-cleaning uniform, a purple sash, and a rubber ape mask came running into the living room. It was my father.

He tripped on the edge of one of the living room mattresses and landed on his back on another one. He grunted like an ape and picked himself up.

"Are you coming trick-or-treating with us, Mr. Krinkle?" Patti asked.

"Definitely!" said my father. "I haven't gone trick-or-treating in thirty years. And Cindy's mother is always serving healthy food — I would love some perfectly unhealthy candy!"

If it had been a few weeks earlier, I would have been mortified. But now I thought it was fine if my father came trick-or-treating with us in an ape mask. "Let's hit the streets!" I said.

We started out at the Armstrongs' house next door.

"Trick or treat!" said Patti as she rang the bell.

"Trick or treat!" said my father in an ape grunt.

Mrs. Armstrong came to the door. "I know that's you, Cindy," she said. "I can tell by the freckles on your nose. And I know that's you, little Patti. But who's the tall one in the ape mask with the long hair sticking out?"

"It's me, Smith Krinkle," my father grunted.

"Oh," said Mrs. Armstrong. She gave Patti and me candy bars.

"What about me?" my father asked.

Mrs. Armstrong gave him a candy bar and a funny look. The three of us giggled and went next door to the Laceys'.

Mr. Lacey said: "Hi there, everybody. It's nice of

you to keep an eye on the girls, Smith."

"I came along for the candy," my father said.

Mr. Lacey laughed and winked at my father. "I'd go trick-or-treating myself if I had the nerve," he said. "But I don't." He gave each of us a lollipop, a candy bar, and three pennies for charity.

The people next to the Laceys were new in the neighborhood. My father introduced us to the lady who answered the door: "Hi, I'm Smith Krinkle. The Empire State Building here is my daughter, Cindy. The little surprise package is her friend, Patti."

"Nice to meet you," the lady said. "I'm Deborah Roth." She gave us some candy. "This seems to be a fun neighborhood to live in," Mrs. Roth said.

"Yes, it is," said my father. Then he ran down the driveway like an ape. Patti and I laughed and ran after him. It's not easy to run when you're wearing surprise package and Empire State Building costumes.

On our way to the next house, we saw two little boys. One was dressed like a monster and the other was dressed like a robot. They were both crying.

My father took off his mask so he wouldn't scare them. "What's wrong?" he asked.

"Two big boys threw eggs at us," said the little boy dressed like a robot.

"They're hiding behind bushes on Oak Street," said the monster.

My father reached into the pocket of his airplane-cleaning uniform and took out a clean rag. He wiped the egg off the little boys' costumes. "It's terrible of those boys to ruin your Halloween," he said. "Let's make sure they don't spoil anyone else's holiday." My father thought for a minute, and then he told us what to do . . .

My father, the two little boys, Patti, and I walked to Oak Street. We hid behind some bushes across the street from where the big boys were hiding. The moonlight was bright enough for us to see them. They were both dressed like pirates, with mean-looking masks. They didn't see us.

My father put on his mask and walked across the street very slowly. He sneaked up right behind the boys and started grunting very loudly. The boys screamed. They screamed more when they turned around and saw a big ape-man waving his arms and grunting at them. They tried to run away, but my father had them cornered in the bushes.

The boys kept screaming, and my father kept grunting and moving around like an angry ape. Patti, the robot, the monster, and I were laughing. I laughed especially hard when one of the big boys' masks fell off. It was Roger Snooterman!

My father finally stopped grunting. He took off his ape mask and yelled for us to come over.

When we walked across the street, Roger Snooterman and his friend, Andy Something-or-Other, were standing there, shaking.

"You boys ought to be ashamed of yourselves for throwing eggs," my father said. He took the rest of their eggs away from them. "Halloween is a wonderful holiday, and you have made these young children miserable and afraid," he said. "That's why I decided to make *you* miserable and afraid for a few minutes."

"I'm sorry," Roger Snooterman said.

"Me too," Andy Something-or-Other said.

"I'm trying to think how you can make it up to this fine young robot and fine young monster," my father said. "I wish I had my safari hat to help me think better."

"*I* know," Patti said. "Make them hand over their candy!"

"An excellent idea," said my father.

So Roger and Andy emptied their trick-or-treat bags into the little boys' trick-or-treat bags. The little boys seemed to feel a lot better.

My father and the other kids left, but I stayed behind to talk to Roger Snooterman for a minute. I hadn't seen him since before I went on the Young Blue Jays hike.

Roger didn't act so sorry now that my father wasn't around. "I know it's you under that paper-bag mask, Cindy Krinkle," he said. "Aren't you embarrassed to have your weirdo father running around in an ape mask?"

"Let me tell you something, Roger Snooterman," I said. "My family may be weird, but I'd much rather have them be weird than mean like you. I'll tell you something else — you're one of the only people in the world who doesn't appreciate my family. And to tell you the truth, I don't care what sourpusses like you think anyway!"

Roger Snooterman didn't know what to say to that.

"She told you, all right!" Andy Something-or-Other said.

I wondered why I had ever worried about what Roger Snooterman thought of my family.

I caught up with my father, Patti, the robot, and the monster halfway down Oak Street. We all went trick-or-treating together.

"We're lucky that you came along, Mr. Krinkle," the robot was saying.

"Cindy and I are lucky too," Patti said. "Those boys might have thrown eggs at us!"

My father just grunted. But I could tell he was smiling under his ape mask.

We went to a whole bunch of houses. We saw lots

of other trick-or-treaters in great costumes. And we got a big haul of candy.

When our trick-or-treat bags got heavy, we decided to go home. My father and I walked the other kids to their houses.

"See you in school tomorrow," Patti, the surprise package, called from her front door. I could see the TV on in her parents' den.

"Thanks for making Halloween so much fun," I said to my father. I kissed him on the rubber cheek of his mask.

"Did you ever see an ape that could pick up the Empire State Building?" asked my father. He picked me up and twirled me around in a circle.

At home, my father and I emptied our trick-or-treat bags onto the dining room table.

"Hey, you got some good stuff!" Sarah said.

"What perfect timing!" said my mother. "I just finished cooking soyburgers. We can eat some of this candy for appetizers."

"Great idea!" I said. "Then we can have the soyburgers for dessert."

We sat around the dining room table and ate our delicious Halloween candy appetizers.

There definitely are advantages to having a weird family.